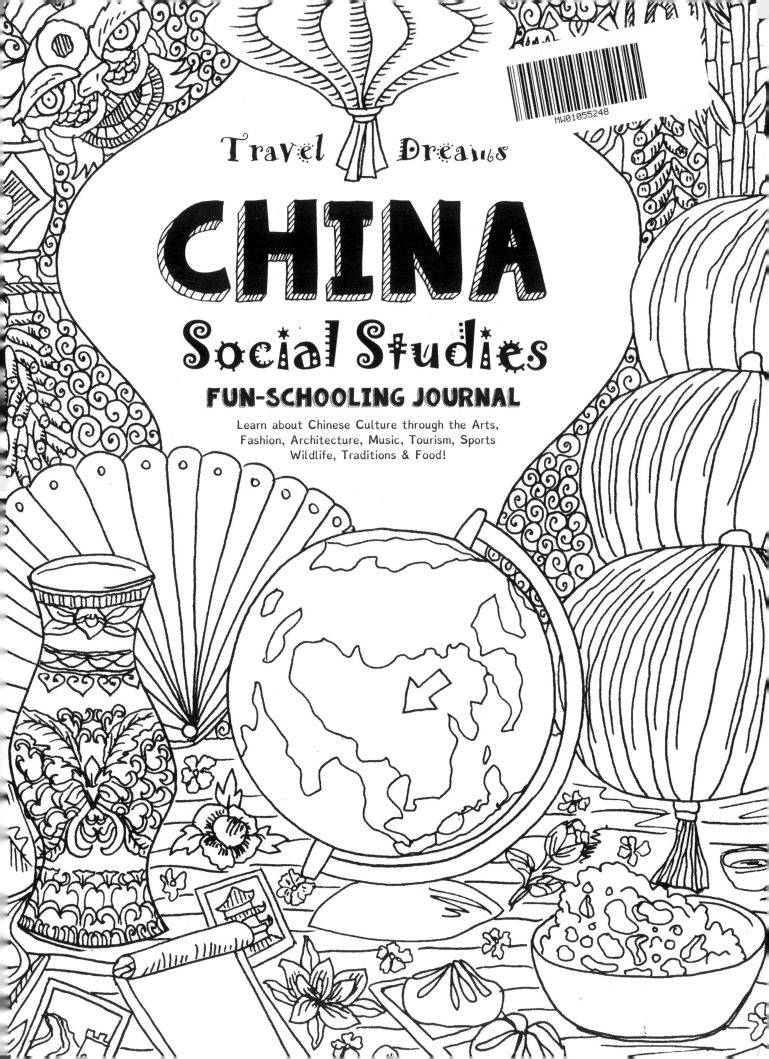

Travel Dreams

CHINA

Social Studies

FUN-SCHOOLING JOURNAL

Learn about Chinese Culture through the Arts,
Fashion, Architecture, Music, Tourism, Sports
Wildlife, Traditions & Food!

MW01055248

To hear traditional music from this country listen to

Travel Dreams
Geography

AROUND THE WORLD
IN 14 SONGS

Search for Amazon Product Number: B072C2QXJS

Around the world in 14 songs is a delightful musical tour of the world. Adults and children will enjoy these original instrumental songs that reflect the authentic style of music that originated on all six major continents. Travel to the rhythm and melody of traditional instruments, and enjoy the fun-filled tunes.

The musical journey begins in Ireland, sweeps across Europe, dances through Asia, Africa and then soars over the ocean to Australia and the Caribbean! After an exciting night at a Smoky Mountain bluegrass festival you will enjoy a siesta in Mexico and finally land in Brazil where you will join the festa in Rio-De-Janeiro.

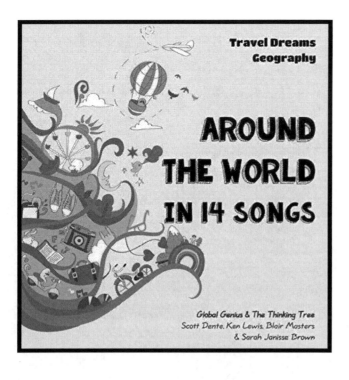

Music has never been more fun... or educational!

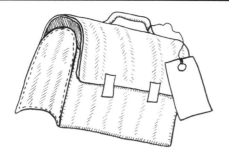

Travel Dreams
CHINA
FUN-SCHOOLING
JOURNAL

An Adventurous Approach
Social Studies

Learn about Chinese Culture Through the Arts,
Fashion, Architecture, Music, Tourism, Sports,
Wildlife, Traditions & Food!

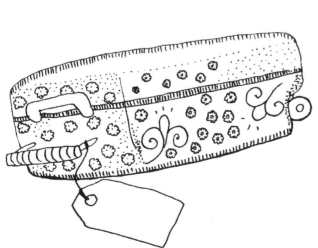

Travel Dreams
CHINA
Fun-Schooling
Journal

Name:

Date:

Contact Information:

About Me:

Let's Learn!

Topics & Activities You Can Explore With This Curriculum:

- Ethnic Cooking
- Travel
- History of Interesting Places
- How People Live
- Tourism
- Transportation
- Wildlife and Natural Wonders
- Cultural Traditions
- Natural Disasters

- Famous and Interesting People
- Missionary Stories
- Scientific Discoveries
- Fashion
- Architecture
- Plants
- Animals
- Maps
- Language

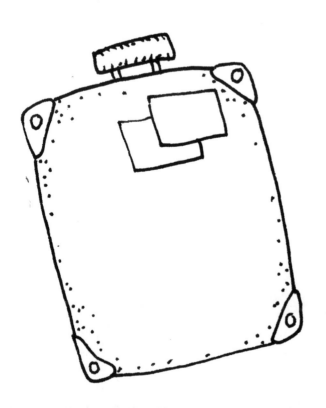

CHINA

Travel Dreams Fun-School Journal

You are going to learn about China

Teacher & Parent To-Do List:

- Plan a trip to China or just plan a trip to the library or local bookstore.
- Download Google Earth so your child can zoom in and learn more!
- Choose online videos about China so your child can learn about culture, food, tourism, traditions and history.
- Be prepared to help your child choose an ethnic recipe and shop for the ingredients.

Go to the Library or Bookstore to Pick Out:

- Books about China
- One Atlas or Book of Maps
- One Colorful Cookbook with Recipes from China

DRAW THE COVER OF YOUR BOOKS!

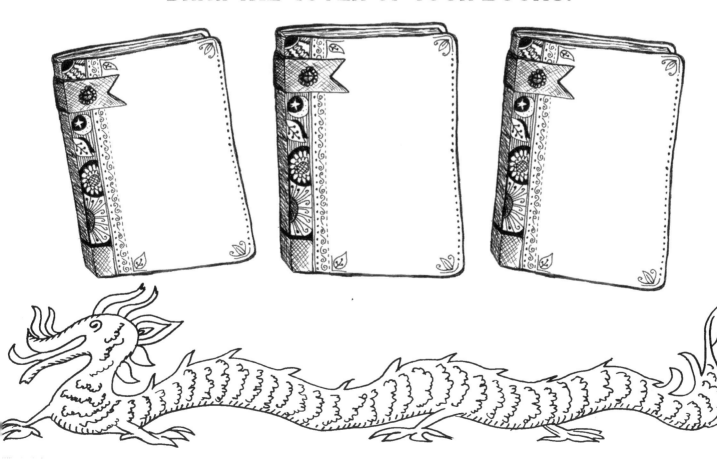

COLOR IN CHINA ON THE MAP

Zoom into China using Google Earth and explore the wonders of this amazing country!

LABEL THE MAP
Add 15 Interesting Things to this Map!

Write or Draw

Use your Library Books

Popular Foods:	Traditional Clothing:
Draw the Flag:	A Quote or Proverb:
A Historic Event:	A Famous Landmark:

LEARNING TIME

READ A BOOK AND WATCH A VIDEO ABOUT FOOD IN CHINA:

BOOK TITLE:_____

_____

VIDEO TITLE: _____

_____

_____

What did you learn?

_____

_____

_____

_____

_____

_____

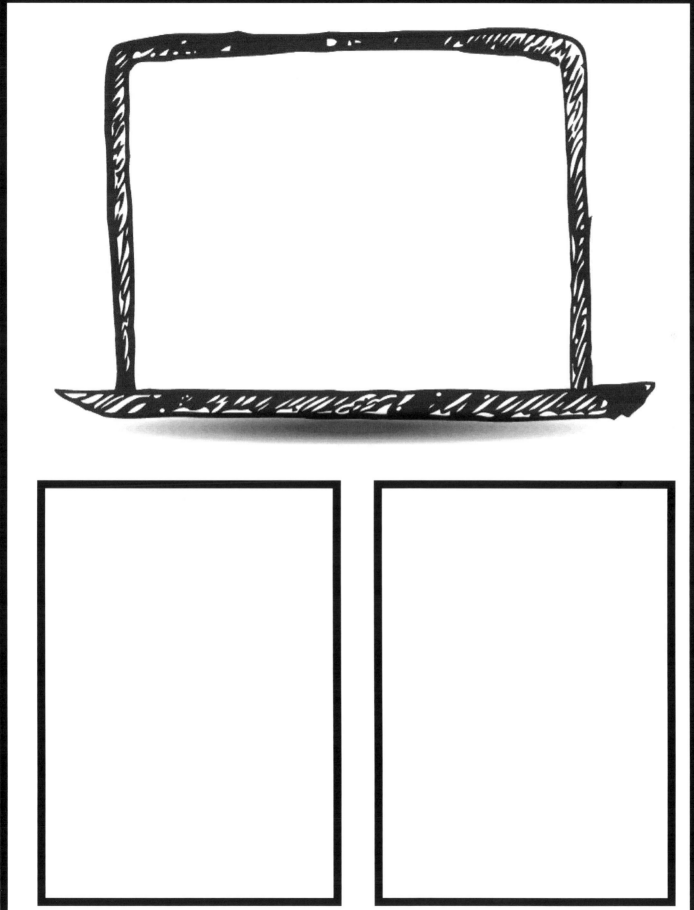

CHINESE CUISINE

WHаT do CHiNeSe peopLe LoVe to eat?

Can you list 5 of the most popular Chinese dishes?

1. _____
2. _____
3. _____
4. _____
5. _____

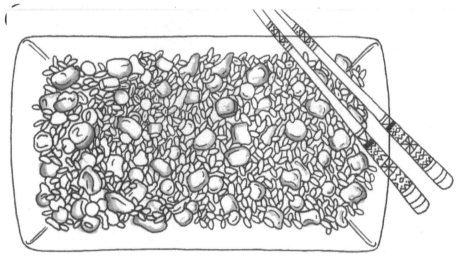

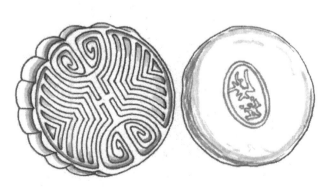

Draw your favorite Chinese food

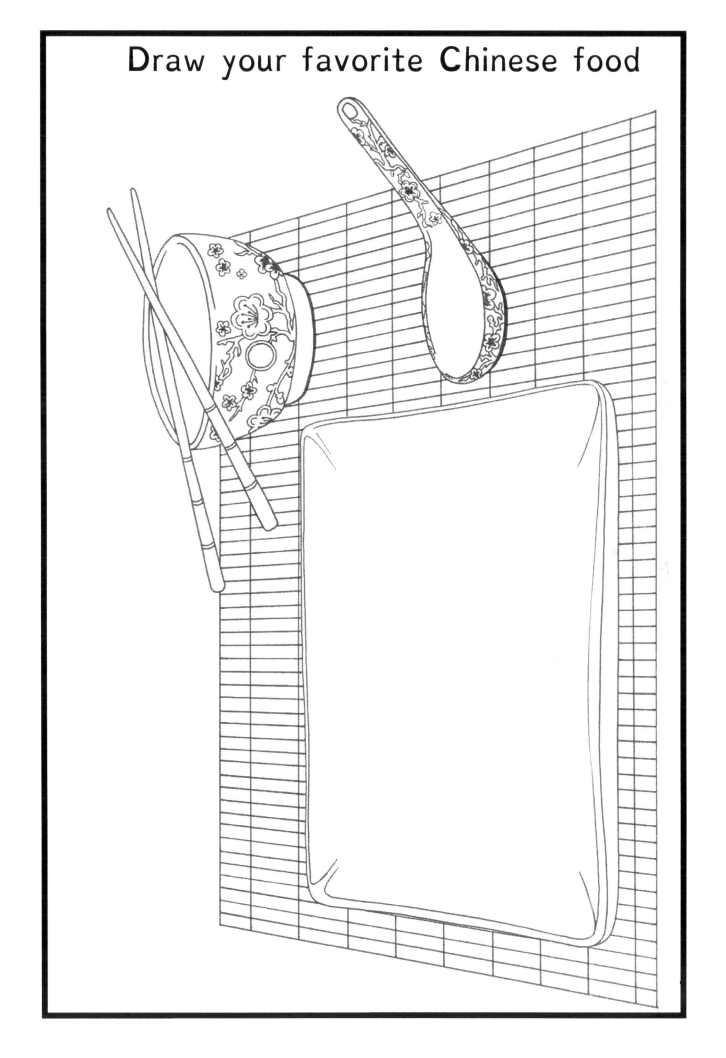

Find a Recipe From
CHINA

TITLE:

_____

Ingredients:

_____   _____

_____   _____

_____   _____

_____   _____

_____   _____

Instructions:

_____

_____

_____

_____

_____

_____

_____

_____

Step by Step Food Prep:

1	2
3	4
5	6

DRAW THE FOOD THAT YOU PREPARED!

RATE THE RESULTS!
1, 2, 3, 4, 5

Color the words that best describe your food:

DELICIOUS

YUMMY

TASTY

GREAT

DELIGHTFUL

OKAY

BLAH!

GROSS

YUCKY

DISGUSTING

STINKY

ICKY

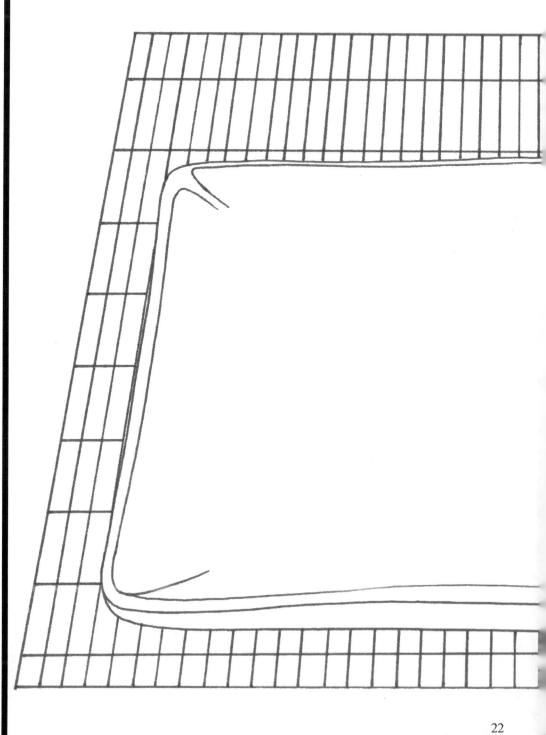

What to Do in China

Create a **COMIC STRIP** showing your dream adventure!

LEARNING TIME

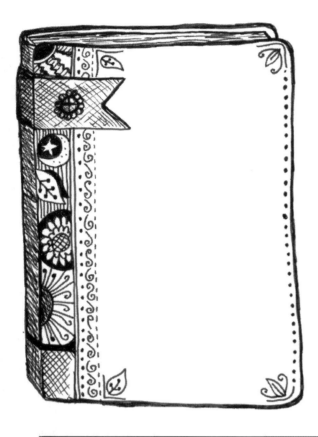

READ A BOOK AND WATCH A VIDEO ABOUT A FAMOUS PERSON

BOOK TITLE:_____
_____
VIDEO TITLE: _____
_____
_____

Write 3 Interesting Biography Facts

_____
_____
_____
_____
_____
_____

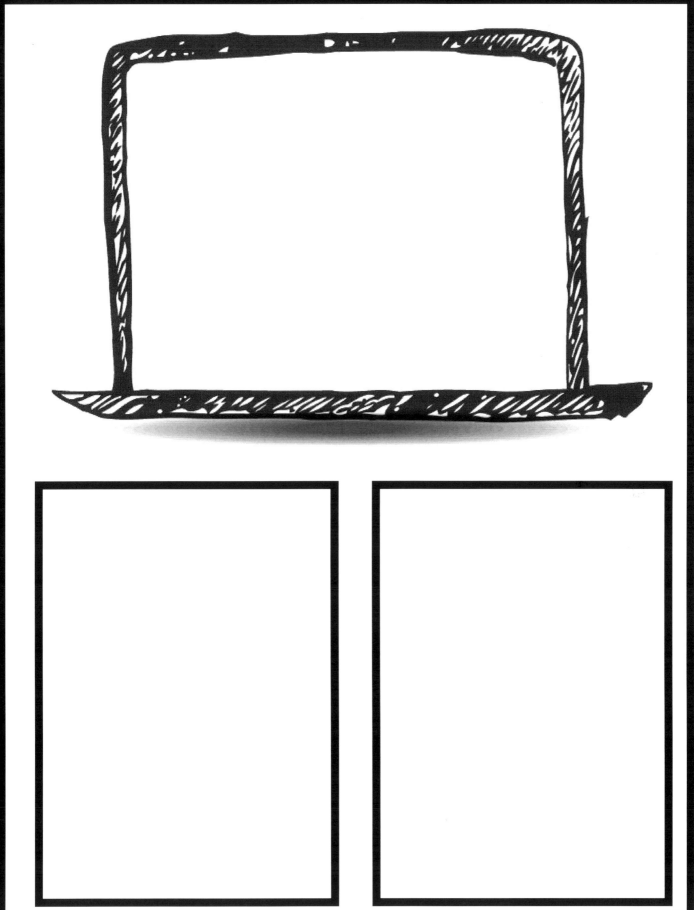

All About Style

CHINA

Fashion in the City

_____

_____

_____

MODERN STYLES

Draw yourself dressed like a stylish Chinese person:

Color The Traditional Costume:

Trace and color this traditional Female Chinese costume

Trace and color this traditional male Chinese costume

CHINESE HISTORY

Write about a Historic Event

LEARNING TIME

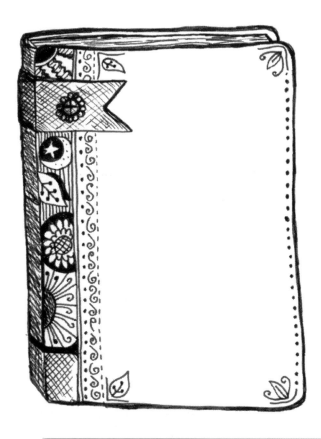

READ A BOOK AND WATCH A VIDEO ABOUT NATURE & WILDLIFE

BOOK TITLE:_____
_____
VIDEO TITLE: _____
_____
_____

Notes:
_____
_____
_____
_____
_____
_____

WHat ANiMaLS LiVe iN CHiNa?
CaN yOU LiSt teN?

1. _____

2. _____

3. _____

4. _____

5. _____

6. _____

7. _____

8. _____

9. _____

10. _____

Draw each of the animals

PLANTS IN CHINA

Can you list ten flowers or trees found in China?

1._____

2._____

3._____

4._____

5._____

6._____

7._____

8._____

9._____

10._____

Draw each of the plants

HISTORY OF MUSIC IN CHINA

Write about a famous Chinese musician:

_____

_____

_____

_____

_____

_____

_____

What instrument did he/she play?

_____

Can you draw it?

A NATIONAL INSTRUMENT

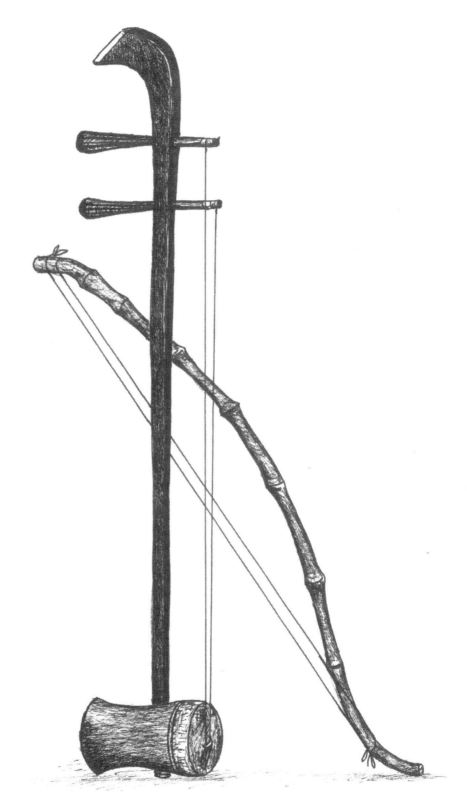

To hear traditional music from this country listen to
Travel Dreams Geography— Around the World in 14 Songs

Track Number & Song Name:
09-China - Dragons, Tigers & Panda Bears

CHINESE ART & ENTERTAINMENT

Read a book or watch a documentary about art and entertainment in China

Write down 5 interesting things you learned :

1. _____

_____

2. _____

_____

3. _____

_____

4. _____

_____

5. _____

_____

Draw or doodle in Chinese Style

Write doWN a quote or a Lyric FroM a FaMous CHiNeSe poeM or SoNg

_____

_____

_____

_____

_____

_____

_____

_____

_____

_____

_____

_____

_____

_____

_____

_____

HISTORY OF TRANSPORTATION IN CHINA

Find 3 interesting Facts about Chinese transportation

1. _____

_____

_____

2. _____

_____

_____

3. _____

_____

_____

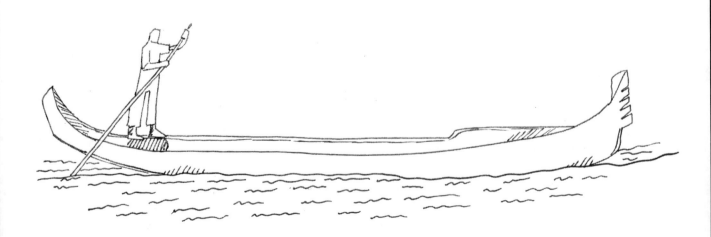

Use your imagination and add something to this picture.

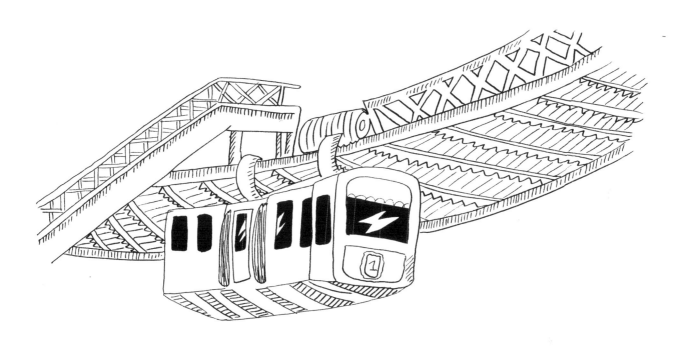

Write a short story about this picture

_____

_____

_____

_____

_____

_____

_____

_____

_____

CHINESE INVENTIONS

Read a book or watch a documentary about your favorite Chinese inventor:

_____

Write down 5 interesting things about his/her life:

1._____

_____

2._____

_____

3._____

_____

4._____

_____

5._____

_____

Write down 3 Chinese inventions that changed the world:

1. _____

2. _____

3. _____

DraW your Favorite CHiNeSe iNVeNTioN

CHINESE SPORTS

Read a book or Watch a documentary about your Favorite Chinese Sport:

_____

Write down 5 interesting things about this Sport

1. _____
_____

2. _____
_____

3. _____
_____

4. _____
_____

5. _____
_____

DraW your Favorite CHiNeSe Sport

CHINESE HOMES
Write about a Family tradition in China

_____

_____

_____

_____

CHINESE TRADITIONS
Draw some traditional Chinese décor elements

Trace & Color
A TRADITIONAL CHINESE HOME

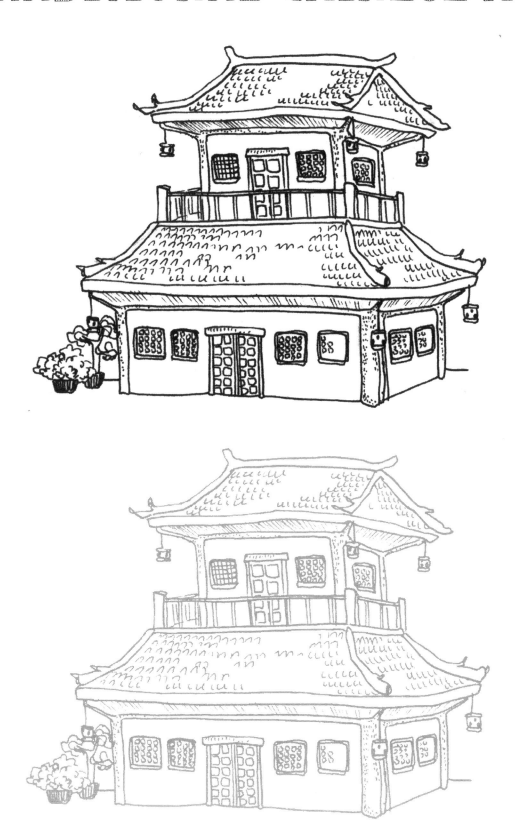

Design Your Own
CHINESE HOME

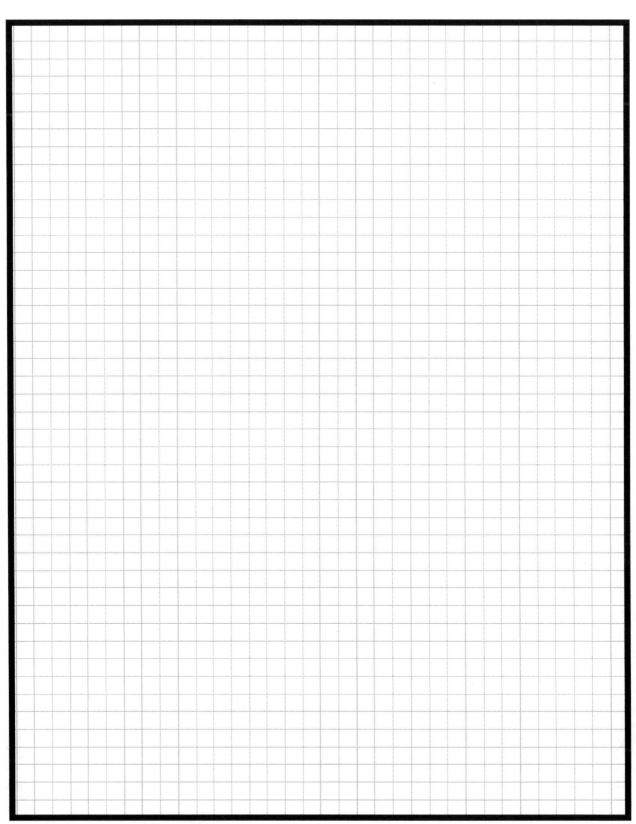

Find and color in the hidden objects

53

LEARNING TIME

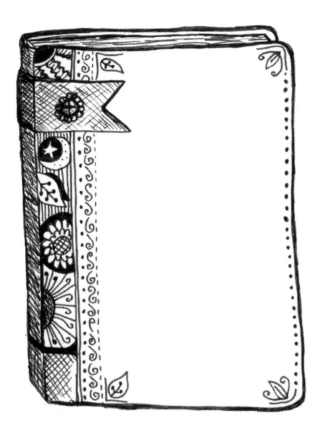

READ A BOOK AND WATCH A VIDEO ABOUT TOURISM & TRAVEL

BOOK TITLE:_____
_____
VIDEO TITLE: _____
_____
_____

Notes:
_____
_____
_____
_____
_____
_____

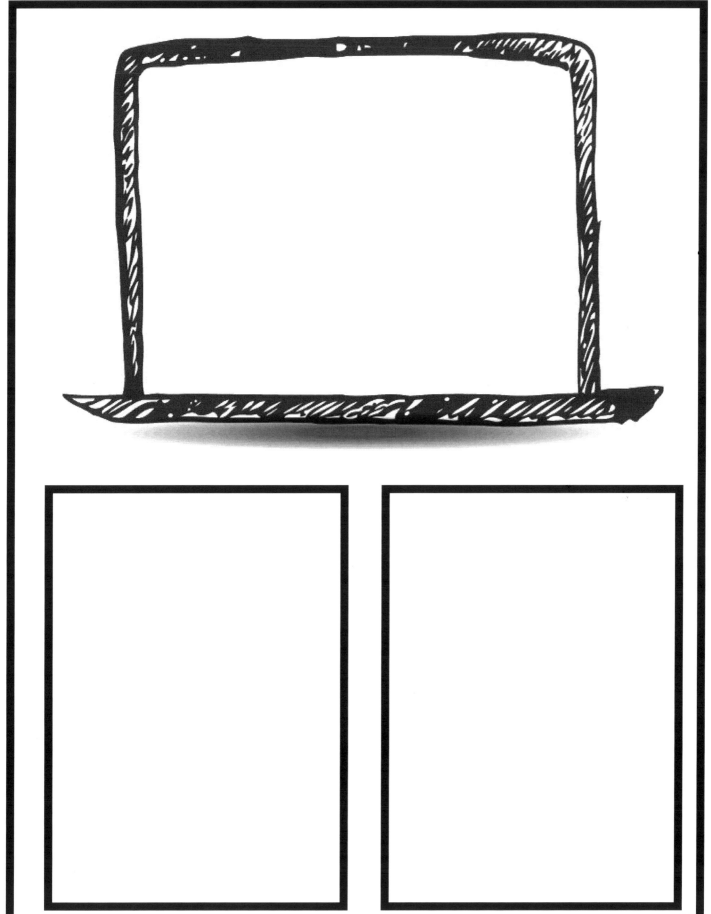

PLAN A TRIP TO THE CAPITAL OF CHINA

- - - - - - - -

Who are you going with?

_____

What are you taking with you?

_____

How long is your trip?

_____

What do you want to see or visit?

_____

PLAN YOUR TRIP

What to Do in Beijing

Five Things to Know
when Traveling to
CHINA

1 _____

2 _____

3 _____

4 _____

5 _____

What to Say

Create a **COMIC STRIP** using six Chinese words:

CREATIVE WRITING

Write a story about an imaginary trip to China

Illustrate your Story

Do It Yourself
HOMESCHOOL
JOURNALS
BY THE THINKING TREE, LLC

Made in the USA
Las Vegas, NV
23 May 2021